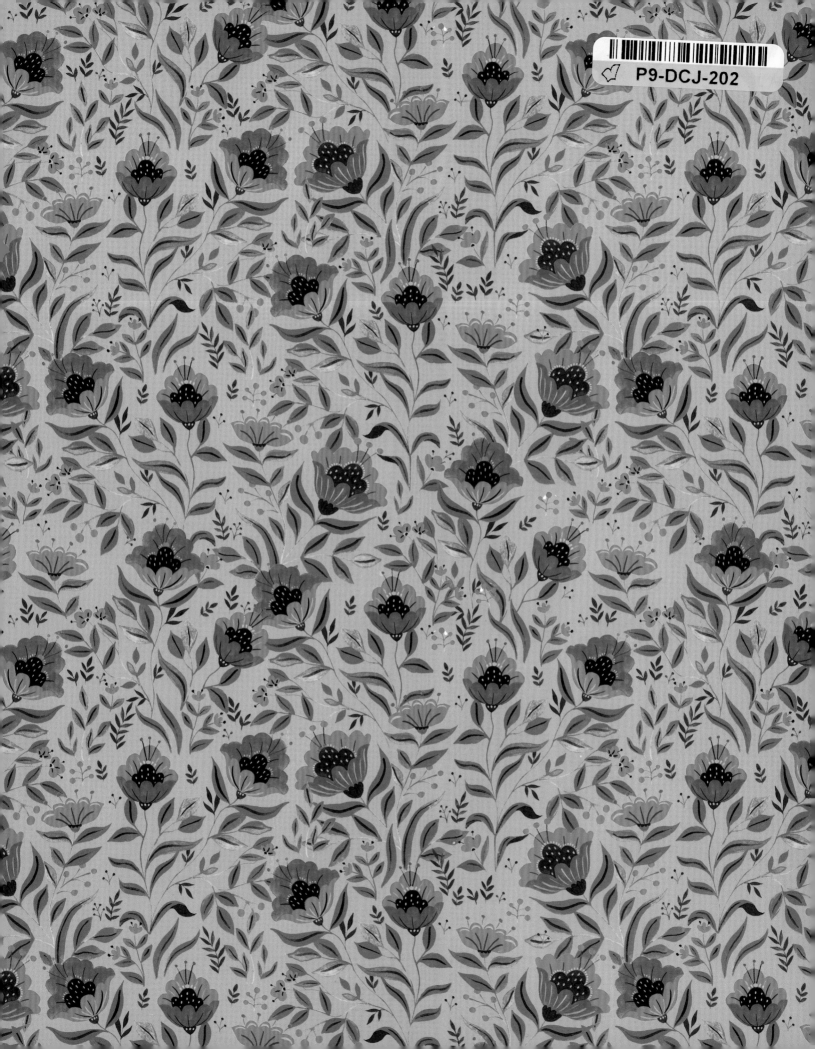

To Pa and Mum

—R. G.

To Sabrina and Babulya Feruza

—D. M.

SALAAM
READS

An imprint of Simon & Schuster Children's Publishing Division
1230 Avenue of the Americas, New York, New York 10020
Text copyright © 2019 by Rukhsanna Guidroz
Illustrations copyright © 2019 by Dinara Mirtalipova
SALAAM READS is a trademark of Simon & Schuster, Inc.
For information about special discounts for bulk purchases, please contact Simon & Schuster Special
Sales at 1-866-506-1949 or business@simonandschuster.com.
The Simon & Schuster Speakers Bureau can bring authors to your live event. For more information or
to book an event, contact the Simon & Schuster Speakers Bureau at
1-866-248-3049 or visit our website at www.simonspeakers.com.
Book design by Lizzy Bromley
The text for this book was set in Incognito.
The illustrations for this book were rendered in gouache on paper.
Manufactured in China • 0419 SCP • First Edition
2 4 6 8 10 9 7 5 3 1
Library of Congress Cataloging-in-Publication Data
Names: Guidroz, Rukhsanna, author. | Mirtalipova, Dinara, illustrator.
Title: Leila in saffron / Rukhsanna Guidroz ; illustrated by Dinara Mirtalipova.
Description: First edition. | New York : Salaam Reads, {2019} | Summary: Shy and unsure of
herself, Leila discovers all the things that make her special with the loving help of her Naani.
Identifiers: LCCN 2018029564 (print) | LCCN 2018040423 (ebook) | ISBN 9781534425644
(hardcover) | ISBN 9781534425651 (Ebook)
Subjects: | CYAC: Pakistani Americans—Fiction. | Self-acceptance—Fiction.
Classification: LCC PZ7.1.G864 (ebook) | LCC PZ7.1.G864 Le 2019 (print) | DDC {E}—dc23
LC record available at https://lccn.loc.gov/2018029564

Leila in Saffron

Rukhsanna Guidroz

Illustrated by Dinara Mirtalipova

SALAAM
READS

New York   London   Toronto   Sydney   New Delhi

Clink, clink.
The song of Naani's glass bangles
welcomes Mom, Dad, and me to her home.

The scent of sweet nutty ghee greets us as soon as the door swings open. We share a family dinner at Naani's every Friday.

Tonight she wears a pale blue silk scarf.
The saffron beads on my dress catch her eye.
"Saffron is a good color for you, Leila.
It suits your dark eyes." Naani strokes
my cheek and smiles.

Sometimes I'm not sure if I like
being me. When I look in a mirror,
I see skinny arms and knobby knees.
But my heart warms when I hear
Naani's words.

Tonight I'm on the lookout for parts of me that I like.

I spy my cousins, uncles, and aunts. They're sitting cross-legged on the living room floor.

"Assalamualaikum," they say.

"Waalaikumsalaam," we chorus back.

Being with my whole family makes me feel snug and happy inside.

My mother says I look just like my aunt did when she was little. I can see it when my aunt smiles. We smile the same!

Pakistani ornaments fill the shelves.
My favorite is a herd of shiny brass
camels. They're all lined up as if ready
for a trek over desert sand dunes.

Books written in Arabic fill the shelves. Their ink makes a curly snail's trail. Mom and Dad help me read the words.

I can't wait for my first trip to Pakistan. I'll get to buy my own special ornaments and Arabic books to bring back home.

I follow Naani into the kitchen.
I love to help make the curry.
I spoon out a rainbow of spices.

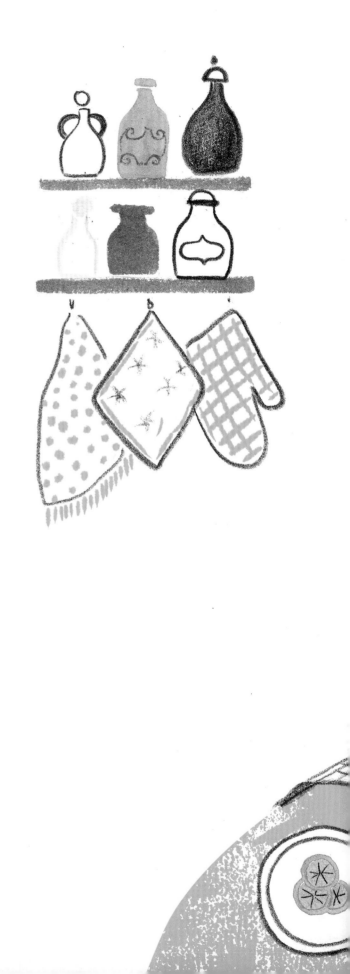

Naani slices onions, garlic, and ginger for the chicken. They go in my rainbow. Wait! We forgot cilantro!

I know where we can find some.

"Hi, Miguel, do you have any cilantro?"
"Of course!" says Miguel.
We head over to his garden, which reminds
me of my strawberry patch at home. I see
his garden has lots of weeds too!

Miguel pulls a bunch of fresh cilantro from his garden and hands it to me. "I know your curry isn't the same without it, Leila."

"Thanks, Miguel." I hurry back to the kitchen.

Everyone in my family enjoys our dinner of chicken curry and warm chapattis. "Delicious!" says Dad. "Leila, your curries are the best!" When everyone agrees, a wave of pride washes over me.

Soon Mom gets ready to leave.
"Challo, bheti," she says.
Time to go already? But I'm still
searching.

Before we go, Naani
invites me upstairs.

She points to a trunk with leather skin wrinkled like a walnut shell. When I lift the lid, it groans. Bundles of silk scarves shimmer before my eyes! I see the color of lentils, bright and orange; pomegranates, juicy and rosy; cucumber skin, dark and green; and threads of saffron, gold and copper.

"Can I try one on?"
I spot my favorite one.
"Of course, Leila.
Here, I'll help you."
In front of the
mirror, I squeeze
my eyes shut. I like
surprises.

Smooth silky fabric tickles my skin.
Naani stands back and says, "Are you ready to see?"

"Wow!" My reflection surprises me.
"What do you see, Leila?"
I see a beautiful girl dressed in a sweet saffron scarf.

When I fix my eyes on my reflection, my words come spilling out. "I see me! I see Leila!"

I slowly spin and notice how I sparkle and shine.
Each and every part of me comes together to make
me who I am.

Glossary

assalamualaikum
(phrase)
(pronounced
ah-sah-LAHM-oo-LAY-come):
peace be with you

bheti
(n.)
(pronounced BEH-ty):
literally "daughter"
but can be used as a term
of endearment such
as "dear" or "sweetie"

challo
(phrase)
(pronounced CHUL-low):
let's go